S0-BAC-084

SEAS
SAVING SPACE ONE PLANET AT A TIME

Star Girl is first published in the United States in 2015
by Picture Window Books
A Capstone imprint
1710 Roe Crest Drive
North Mankato, Minnesota 56003
www.capstonepub.com



Library of Congress Cataloging-in-Publication Data is available on the Library of Congress website.

ISBN: 978-1-4795-8276-1 (library binding)
ISBN: 978-1-4795-8280-8 (paperback)
ISBN: 978-1-4795-8472-7 (eBook PDF)

Summary: Planet Plantagan's air is being polluted, and the vine aliens are suffering. When the space cadets investigate, they get themselves into one big tangle. Can they trust each other enough to save the planet and its inhabitants?

Designer: Natascha Lenz

This *Odd One Out* US Edition is published by arrangement with Macmillan Education Australia Pty Ltd, 15 - 19 Claremont Street, South Yarra, Vic 3141, Australia

Printed in the United States of America by Corporate Graphics

# ODD ONE OUT

LOUISE PARK

PICTURE WINDOW BOOKS
a capstone imprint

# SPACE EDUCATION

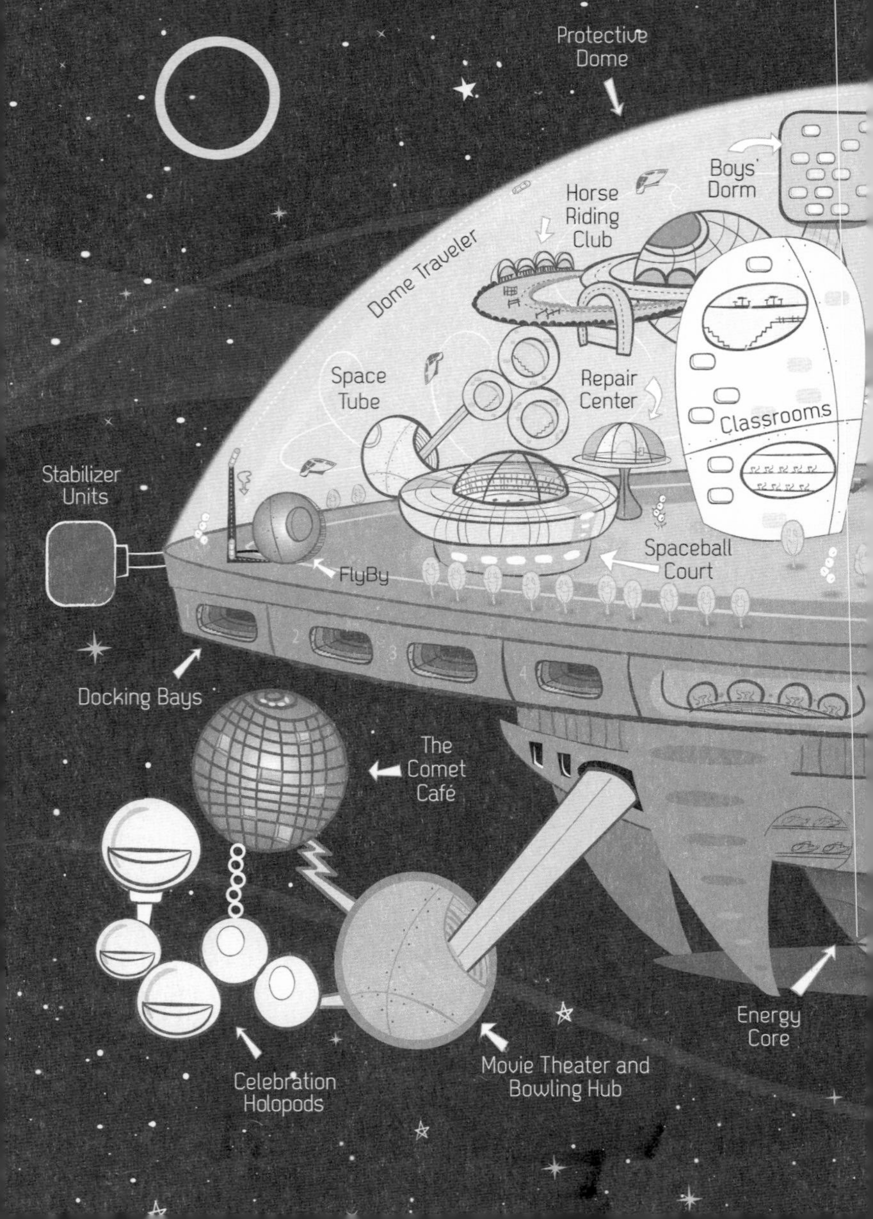

Protective Dome

Boys' Dorm

Horse Riding Club

Dome Traveler

Space Tube

Repair Center

Classrooms

Stabilizer Units

FlyBy

Spaceball Court

1

2

3

4

Docking Bays

The Comet Café

Celebration Holopods

Movie Theater and Bowling Hub

Energy Core

# AND ACTION SCHOOL

# SEAS

## A SPACE STATION BOARDING SCHOOL FOR GIRLS AND BOYS

The Space Education and Action School is located on Space Station Edumax. Students in the space training program complete space missions on planets in outer space that are in danger and need help.

Not all students will make it through to their final year and only the best students will go on to become space agents. Addie must make it through and become a Space Agent. Outer space needs her.

# CONFIDENTIAL
## STAFF ONLY

**Program:** Space Cadetship

**Student:** Adelaide Banks

**Space Cadet:** Star Girl

**Age:** 10 years old

**School house:** Stellar

**Space missions:** 1

**Earned mission points:** 4

**Earned house points:** 75

**Comments:** Adelaide has lost points for breaking an important school rule. Removal of a tracking chip is a serious offense. She also has yet to join any team-based school sports. This behavior may indicate she is not a team player and may not have the makings of a good space cadet. We will need to watch her closely on missions and in class.

# CHAPTER ONE

"We better finish getting ready, Addie," said Olivia. "I don't know what happened to Miya. She wasn't in Space 101 class this afternoon. But we'll be late and it's the first ballet lesson of the term." Olivia was in Miya and Addie's dorm room. She'd come over to get ready for ballet with Addie. Addie had only been at the school for five weeks. And this wasn't just her first ballet lesson of the term. It was her first ballet lesson at her new space station boarding school.

Olivia began pulling Addie's hair up into a tight bun.

"Ouch! Don't pull so hard," Addie said.

"Sorry, Ads," Olivia said. "But you don't have hair that likes to stay in a neat bun."

"I know." Addie laughed. "Mom always used to say my hair had gremlins in it."

Olivia felt really sad that Addie didn't have her mom anymore. She stopped tugging on Addie's hair. She didn't know what to say. She never did when Addie brought up her mom. "Your mom would love that you're at SEAS and training to be a space agent," she said finally.

"I guess so," said Addie, shrugging. "Mom died when I was five, so I don't really know what she would think." Addie changed the subject. "Hey, I'm just going to send a quick message to Miya and see where she is."

Addie took out her SpaceBerry. Every Cadet at SEAS had a SpaceBerry. It was a cell phone and a computer. Addie loved using hers to send text messages to her friends.

ADDIE
Where R U? We are almost ready to go.

MIYA
Just got back from a mission. I'll C U there.

"She was on a mission," Addie said. "Come on, do you have your ballet bag?"

"Yeah, but aren't you going to change out of that purple tutu first?" Olivia asked.

"What do you mean?" asked Addie.

"This is my ballet tutu. It's what I wore to class at home. And I love it!"

"But it's purple!" Olivia said. "Pink is the school color here. Why didn't you get one when you bought your uniforms?"

"I like this one. And I didn't need a new one," Addie said quietly. "And everything cost so much and . . ." She sat down on the bed. "I'm going to look dumb, aren't I?"

"A little," Olivia said. "Come on, we have to hurry or we'll miss the space tube."

Addie usually loved riding on the space tube. It was an overhead rocket pod rail system that went from one part of the space station to any other part. But today Addie felt like the odd one out.

*Pink tutus everywhere,* she thought. She knew everyone was looking at her and whispering. She stared out into space through the dome. Looking out from the pod and seeing all the stars and galaxies was the best part of riding the space tube.

The rocket pod pulled in at the gymnasium and ballet hall and everyone climbed out and went into the studio's lobby. Then Addie heard a voice behind her.

"Hey, new girl," Valentina called out. She was snickering and pointing at Addie's tutu. "I don't think Ms. Styles will be happy to see you wearing that. I hope you lose school house points for Stellar."

Addie knew Valentina didn't like her, but

she thought after their mission together that things might have changed.

Addie smoothed down the purple netting of her skirt. "It's a tutu just like everyone else's," she said. "So what if it's purple?"

"What makes you think you're so special?" said the girl standing with Valentina. "You can't just wear whatever you want."

Addie looked at the girl and was shocked to see that it was Grace. *She showed me around the school when I first arrived,* thought Addie. *She was so friendly to me that day. Why is she being so mean now?*

Addie tried to smile. "Hi, Grace," she said. "I don't think I'm special. This is just my tutu from my old school, that's all."

Suddenly Ms. Styles was behind them, clapping her hands. “Valentina,” she said, “your gym class is starting without you. Off you go.” Then she turned to Addie. “You must be Adelaide Banks. You aren’t wearing the regulation school tutu, Adelaide. I heard that you don’t always follow the school rules. Why aren’t you in pink?”

“This is the tutu from my old school, Ms. Styles,” Addie said. “It’s the only one I have.”

“I see,” said Ms. Styles, softening. “Please see me after class and we’ll figure something out. I’m sure I can find something for you.” She smiled, then ushered the girls into the studio.

“What did she mean about me not

following the school rules?" Addie whispered to Olivia. Olivia shrugged.

"First position and eyes to the front, please," said Ms. Styles.

Ms. Styles led the group through some warm-up exercises, and then they began practicing their leaps. "Push off from the floor and jump," called Ms. Styles. "I want to see you spring from the floor." Then she made the class stop. "Adelaide and Grace, could you come to the front, please, and show the class what a real leap looks like."

Addie groaned. *It's bad enough that I'm in this purple tutu,* she thought. *Now I have to stand in front of the class. And with Grace, who thinks I think I'm trying to be special.*

They went to the front.

"Adelaide, you first, please," said Ms. Styles. Addie pushed off from the floor. "Wonderful leaps, Adelaide," said Ms. Styles. "You should try out for the school spaceball team. Now you, Grace." But before Grace got to jump, a SpaceBerry went off at the back of the room.

"Sounds like someone's wanted for a mission," said Ms. Styles. "Everybody go and check your SpaceBerries, and please be quick." But just then another SpaceBerry went off.

Ding Dong... Ding Dong...

*That's mine,* thought Addie. *Great, another mission. I wonder who I'll be going with?*

Just then Grace held up her SpaceBerry. "It's me, Ms. Styles."

"And me," Addie added.

"Well, no more leaps for you two today," said Ms. Styles. "Off you go to the FlyBy. Have a safe mission, girls."

# CHAPTER ★ TWO

The FlyBy was way over on the other side of the space station.

"We'll take the dome traveler," said Grace. "It's the fastest way there."

The dome traveler transported people across the inner surface of the space station's dome.

"I haven't been on the dome traveler before," said Addie. "It looks kind of scary."

"It feels like being on a rollercoaster," said Grace. "You kind of stick to the roof and slide along it from one side to the other. You stand in between the guides, and when the activate button is pushed, you'll be sucked against the dome and held there for the entire ride."

The girls stepped into the dome travelers and pressed their backs against the surface.

"It's kind of like a glass elevator at home," said Addie.

"Except there are no doors," said Grace.

"Oh," said Addie, feeling a little sick. "And we won't fall out?"

"No one has yet, but there's a first time for everything. Ready?" asked Grace.

"Ready as I'll ever be," said Addie. "So how do we work this thing?"

"See the control panel? Hit the FlyBy button and then the one that says activate," said Grace, hitting hers and whizzing off.

Addie nervously hit the buttons. There was a strange sucking sound. She was pulled tightly against the dome. Then she shot up along the inside of the dome and slid down the other side, coming to a stop on the ground near the FlyBy.

"So what did you think?" asked Grace.

"It's great!" Addie said. "Seeing the whole space station from up there was unreal! It made my stomach feel a little funny though. I thought I was going to be sick when I hit the highest part of the dome."

"Good thing you didn't," said Grace.

The girls walked over to the mission briefing room door. “You go first,” Addie said.

Grace stepped up to the small screen on the door and smiled. Then Addie did the same. Words flashed on the security screen.

The door opened and they went inside.

The briefing room was buzzing with activity. The girls' dorm teacher stood facing one of the screens.

“Hello, Mrs. Lamrock,” the girls said.

She turned to Grace and Addie.

"You made good time, girls," she said. "Good work. I will be briefing you for this mission and I will be the mission holograph teacher. How's your new roommate working out, Adelaide?"

"Really, really well. Thanks, Mrs. Lamrock," Addie said, feeling a little awkward about that whole situation with Valentina.

"Good," said Mrs. Lamrock. "Hopefully things will go smoother on this mission too."

Addie flinched. *Things weren't that bad on the last mission, were they?*

She liked Mrs. Lamrock. When Addie had been homesick the dorm teacher had been kind. She thought about saying something about her first mission but decided against it. Instead she said, "Mrs. Lamrock . . . um . . . well, everyone at home just calls me Addie. And so do my friends. Would it be all right if the teachers called me Addie too?" It was the first time she felt comfortable enough to ask a teacher something like that.

"I'll make a note of that, Addie," Mrs. Lamrock said with a smile. "Now, we need to send you girls to Planet Plantagan."

"I studied Plantagan's galaxy in Space 101 last term," said Grace. "It's so far away."

"That's right, it is," said Mrs. Lamrock. "Space Agent Space Surfer will be taking you, and he knows a few shortcuts. He'll have you there with plenty of time for you to complete your mission."

"What will we be traveling in?" asked Addie. She remembered Valentina asking the same question on their last mission. Addie wanted Grace to know she had a partner who knew about missions.

"I'll show you," said Mrs. Lamrock. "Come this way and I'll brief you on board."

Mrs. Lamrock took the girls back into the FlyBy area. Bots were busy working, and space pods and shuttles were coming and going.

"But this is where we get dropped off when we come back from breaks," said Grace. "There are usually only school shuttles here."

"You're right," said Mrs. Lamrock. "But not everything is the way it seems. You might want to think about that, Comet XS. Here is the space shuttle you will be traveling in. Please climb aboard."

*It's just a school space shuttle,* thought Addie. *Grace is right. How's this going to get us anywhere super fast?*

Then she stepped inside. Grace and Addie looked at each other and laughed. The inside was anything but a school space shuttle. The two hundred student seats were gone, and in their place were just two seats that were almost like beds.

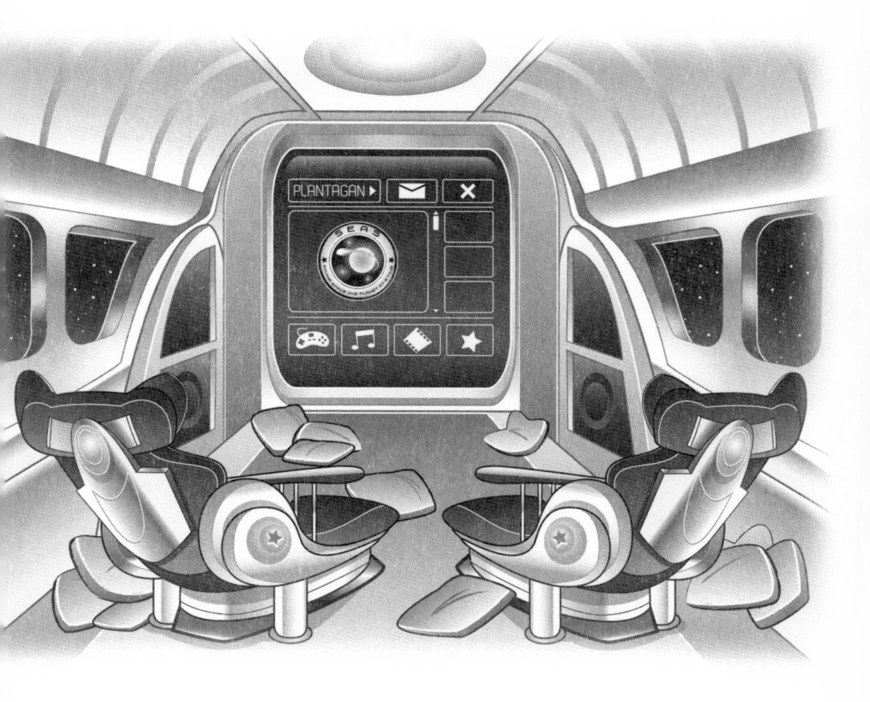

There was a pile of soft cushions and a large touch screen on the wall with select buttons for the latest movies, songs, and games. Mrs. Lamrock touched a button labeled "Plantagan" and an image filled the screen.

"This is Plantagan," said Mrs. Lamrock.

"It looks like a giant jungle," said Addie. "Except it's all blue."

"Yes," said Mrs. Lamrock. "But the forests are usually a much brighter blue. Something is polluting the air there, and all the life forms are suffering. The air is also very poisonous for humans now. We need you girls to investigate and report back. Now, come over to the table so I can take you through your mission equipment."

They all walked over to the table and looked at the equipment.

"These spacesuits will protect you from Plantagan's polluted air," said Mrs. Lamrock.

Addie looked at the shiny silver suits. "They look kind of small."

"The suits are designed to be a close fit," said Mrs. Lamrock. "They're like a second skin so there's nothing loose and flapping on them that can get caught on twigs or branches. You don't want to get a tear out there. The air will burn your skin."

"What are those things?" asked Grace.

"Gas goggles," answered Mrs. Lamrock. "They fit onto your helmets and will allow you to see in all sorts of conditions. The

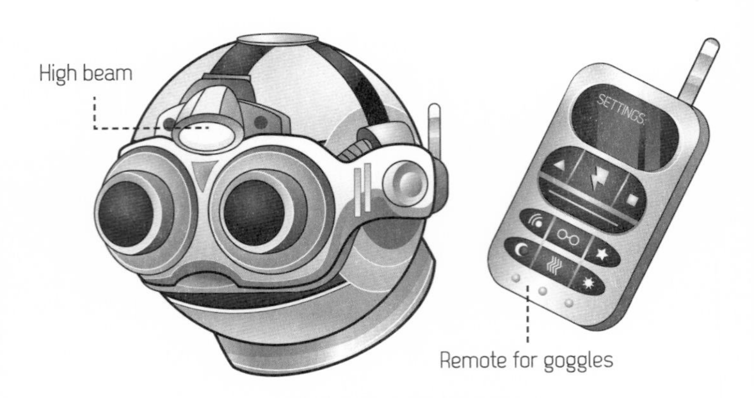


**GAS GOGGLES**

controls and settings for the goggles are in your mission packs. You'll also find rope and oxygen poppers in there too."

The girls opened their mission packs, and they each found what looked just like a party popper with a pull string.

"You only have one each," Mrs. Lamrock continued. "They should be used only in an extreme emergency. Once the string is pulled an oxygen bubble will be released. You will be

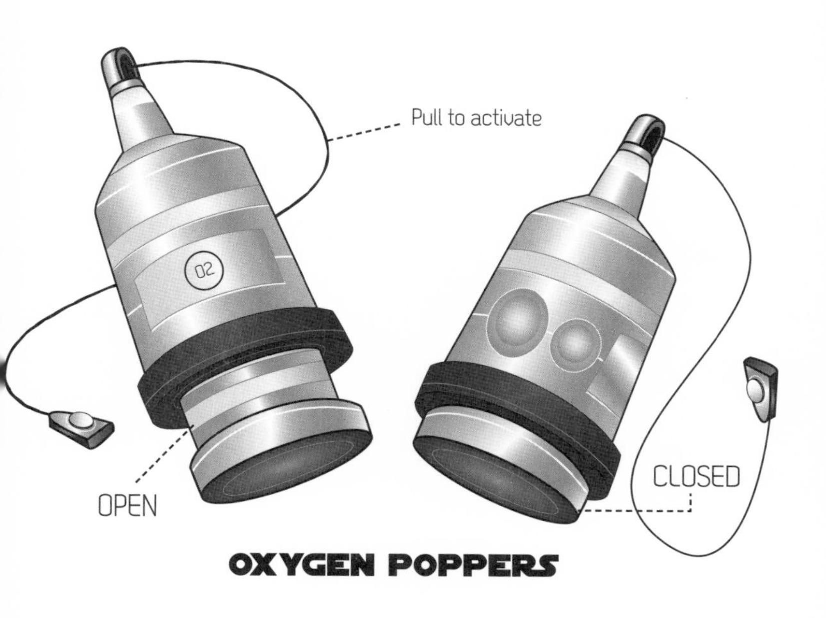


**OXYGEN POPPERS**

protected inside the bubble, and it will give you enough air to breathe while you wait to be rescued. But I'm sure you won't need to use them at all. Now, can I have your watches, please, so that I can check your tracking chips and load myself in as your mission holograph? While I'm doing that, you can use the time to learn all you can about Plantagan. Takeoff will be in ten minutes."

Mrs. Lamrock took the girls' watches and went back into the FlyBy. The girls took out their SpaceBerries and logged on to the school's information site.

"Ten minutes isn't much time," said Addie to Grace. "Why don't you learn about the environment and I'll do the alien life forms?"

"No way," said Grace. "I'll do my own research, thanks."

Addie stared at Grace. "Why not? If we share the—"

"I don't trust you, if you must know."

"Why not?" Addie asked, shocked.

"You're wasting time," Grace said, brushing Addie's question aside. "Let's just get on with the mission and try to earn a good score." She turned back to her SpaceBerry, leaving Addie a little upset. Addie had trouble concentrating but started researching the planet's aliens anyway.

"Time to suit up, girls," said Mrs. Lamrock. "Here are your watches. You know the rules. The tracking chips are to be on at all times. We'll also be able to listen in on the mission with them now, thanks to a new piece of technology in the chip. Before you leave the shuttle, Space Surfer will check that your helmets are on correctly and that your tanks are working. Good luck, girls, and be sure to work as a team."

# CHAPTER ★ THREE

Grace sat in her seat. The girls' helmets, goggles, and tanks were strapped into the holding bays. Addie was still trying to push her ballet clothes into the storage bay.

"Welcome back, Star Girl and Comet XS," said Space Surfer over the shuttle's cabin speakers. "Please make sure everything is stowed and ready for takeoff."

"Ready for takeoff," said Grace clearly, aware that everything that was said in the cabin was transmitted to the cockpit.

Addie ran to her seat, dropping her tutu.

The shuttle's engines roared. The loading dock opened and the shuttle took off.

After about twenty minutes of flying, Grace switched on the screen. "It will probably be a few hours before we reach Plantagan's galaxy. I think I'll watch a movie."

"Wrong, SC Comet XS," said Space Surfer. "Today we'll be taking a little wormhole I know about."

"Wormholes are like shortcuts in space, right?" asked Addie.

"Exactly right, Star Girl," said Space Surfer. "If you look out your cabin window, you'll see the Spanamax Galaxy. We need to be on the other side of it. And it's massive!"

Space Surfer continued, “But the wormhole goes straight through it and drops us right near Plantagan in just minutes.”

The shuttle began to turn. It headed straight for the galaxy.

“Hold on to your seats, space cadets,” said Space Surfer. “Sometimes these wormholes can cause a little spin out!”

Suddenly the scene outside of the window went black. Then the shuttle started to spin.

It went round and round, over and under and up and down. Grace was laughing and enjoying the ride, but Addie's face was as white as the cabin walls.

"It's just like the dome traveler, Addie," said Grace. "You aren't going to be sick, are you?"

"I don't know," said Addie quietly. She shut her eyes tight. "How much longer?"

"Hang in there, Star Girl. We're totally safe," said Space Surfer.

Just when Addie really thought she was going to be sick, the shuttle straightened out and it was over. She opened her eyes and looked out the cabin window. There was a very blue-looking planet in the distance.

"That must be it," she said.

"Get organized, cadets," said Space Surfer. "We'll be landing on Plantagan soon."

Addie got the helmets and goggles from the holding bay, and she and Grace helped each other put them on.

"Be sure to check your mission pack before you clip it around your waist," said Space Surfer. "Buckle up and prepare for landing."

The shuttle touched down on a patch of deep blue grass.

"The air out there is filled with toxic gas," said Space Surfer. "Let's get those oxygen tanks on and checked."

Addie was picking up her oxygen tank when she noticed her purple tutu on the floor. *That's caused enough trouble for one day,* Addie thought. *I don't want Space Surfer seeing it.* She quickly stuffed it into her mission pack.

Space Surfer came down into the cabin to do final checks on the girls' equipment. "You two are good to go," he said as he finished the check. "Step into the exit chamber and I'll let you out. Good luck and good cadeting."

The doors slid open and Addie and Grace stepped inside the chamber. The doors closed behind them, and then after a few seconds the doors in front of them opened. The girls stepped out onto Planet Plantagan.

# CHAPTER FOUR

"This place is just a bunch of dark blue vines, roots, giant plants, and jungle," said Grace. "But it's not supposed to look like this."

"You're right," said Addie. "The plants should all be brighter and lighter. And the air is thick with a green kind of smoke."

The girls took out their goggle remotes and set them to smoke screen.

"Now that I can see better, this place looks sick," said Addie. "And I think I know why. Look at that!"

She pointed to big green clouds of smoke that were billowing up into the sky above the treetops. “We need to find out what that is.”

“And to get there we have to go through that thick blue jungle,” said Grace. She began walking and Addie followed.

At first it wasn’t hard to walk through, but the jungle soon became thicker and thicker.

“Why did you say you don’t trust me?” asked Addie.

“Valentina said you left her on the ice when she fell on the mission with you at Polare,” said Grace. “And she lost points because of what you did with your tracking chip. She’s not the top-scoring space cadet now because of you. I don’t want to get a bad score, that's why I can't afford to trust you."

"I didn't leave her on the ice," said Addie, horrified. "Why would Valentina make up a story like that?"

"It's you who says it's a story," said Grace.

Addie was about to say something about the tracking chip, but Grace stopped her. "Shhhh! Listen. What's that noise?"

HHIIISSSSSS

HHIIISSSSS

"It's the vines," Addie said.

Thick blue vines were sliding down the tree trunks and along the ground like snakes.

HHHHIIIIISSSSSSS

There were vines coming from everywhere. They quickly wrapped around Grace's legs and pulled her to the ground.

"I can't move," Grace shouted. "Do something!"

But Addie was caught too.

Grace still had one hand free. She pulled on the vines around her legs and managed to break one. An eerie noise filled the jungle.

"It's calling for more vines," said Addie. "These alien tree things must think we're here to hurt them. I downloaded an alien translator application on my SpaceBerry, but I can't reach it. My hands are too tied up."

"I have it too," said Grace. "I think I can get my SpaceBerry out."

Grace tried to get her SpaceBerry with her free hand, but the vines were wrapped so thick and tight around her waist that she couldn't undo the zipper on her mission pack.

"It's no good," she said. "I can't get it."

"Try to get mine out," said Addie, and she wriggled as close to Grace as she could.

Grace slowly tugged the zipper open and took out Addie's SpaceBerry. She held the phone in the palm of her hand and activated the translator app with her thumb.

"It worked!" said Grace, and she spoke into the phone. "We are space cadets from SEAS. We are here to help. Please let us go so we can find out what is poisoning your air."

The eerie noises turned into whispers, and the SpaceBerry translated them.

"We will let you pass," the vines said. "But you must go through the mountain. Whatever is poisoning us and our planet is coming from the other side." Then the vines slowly loosened their grip and slithered back to where they'd come from.

The girls slowly stood.

"All good?" asked Grace.

"Yep," said Addie. "Come on, let's hurry."

As the girls walked they could hear the plant-like aliens talking.

OOORRRRAH WOOOOOEEE

They were passing on a message through the jungle. As Addie and Grace made their way to the foot of the mountain, plants parted and vines shrank out of their way.

At the base of the mountain were two openings. One looked very low and small.

The other was almost big enough to walk into.

"I'll check out the big one," Grace told Addie. "You wait here."

Inside, the tunnel was so dark that Grace couldn't see. She took out the remote for her goggles and set them to high beam view. Instantly the tunnel filled with light.

The walls were dripping with a sticky, toxic-looking orange slime. Vine-like aliens fell limply over crevices and rocks. Their multiple eyes were all half closed.

Grace's heart was pumping. She could feel sweat trickling down the back of her neck. She hated being underground and she hated being in small places. *Stay calm,* she told herself. *It's just those alien vines.*

Grace went a little farther until she could see that the tunnel stopped just up ahead. She turned and ran back outside.

"It's no good," she said to Addie, panting. "It's a dead end."

"Are you okay?" Addie asked. "You look worse than I felt going through that wormhole."

"I'm fine," Grace snapped. "Go and try the small tunnel."

Addie had to get down on her hands and knees to fit inside. She started crawling.

It was pitch black, and she could hear her helmet scraping on the roof of the cave. And through her tight spacesuit she could feel something dripping onto her back.

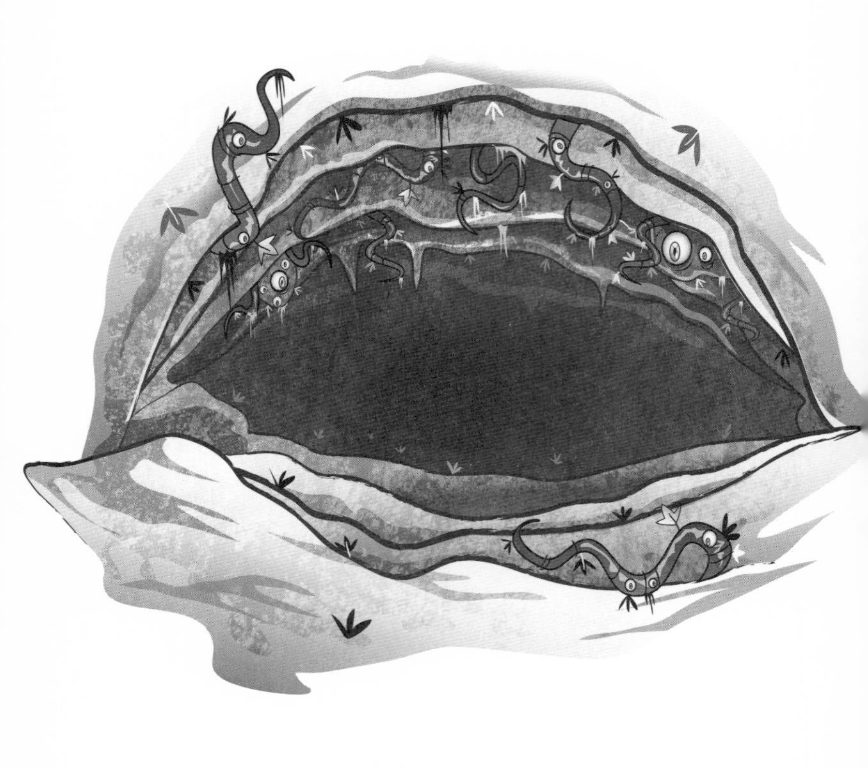

*What is that stuff?* she thought. Addie switched on the high beam on her goggles. Then she saw the sticky orange stuff that Grace had seen. It was dripping from the plant-like aliens onto the ground, making it sticky to crawl on.

Addie looked down the tunnel and could see it went a long way, even though it was really low in places. She crawled backward out of the tunnel to Grace.

"I can see it goes for a long way, and it looks pretty tight in spots," Addie said. "We'll have to crawl all the way. Let's go."

"You go. I'll wait here," said Grace. She looked close to tears.

"Grace, you know we have to stay together. What's wrong?" Addie asked.

Grace bit her lip and was trying hard not to cry. "I get super-weird in small spaces. I freak out! I couldn't cope being in that bigger tunnel, so I can't go in that small one. There's no way. I can't! This mission is over for me. I've ruined everything. I'll never make space agent once the school finds out."

"Well, they won't find out," said Addie. She looked around. *There must be another way,* she thought. But there wasn't. They had to go through the small tunnel. Then Addie remembered something her mom had told her a long time ago.

"Grace, turn off your goggles and close your eyes," she said. "With your eyes shut, you can pretend you are anywhere. Keep your eyes closed all the way and don't open them at all. I'll take you through the tunnel." Addie took out the rope in her mission pack. "I'm going to tie one of my legs to one of your legs. And then I'll tie one of my arms to one of your arms. It'll be just like a three-legged race, but we'll be crawling."

"It won't work. I can't go," said Grace.

"It will work," insisted Addie. "When my mom was sick, they used to put her in these narrow tubes to do special medical tests on her. They were just like tunnels. She hated small spaces and she couldn't go in the tubes. She said she learned that if she shut her eyes before she went in and kept them shut until she came out, she could pretend she was somewhere else. Come on, Grace. At least try it."

Grace closed her eyes, stuck out her arm, and nodded once.

Addie tied her arm to Grace's arm.
Then she tied her leg to Grace's leg.

"Okay, down on our hands and knees, and when I move, you move, just like in a three-legged race."

The girls crawled slowly into the tunnel, Grace with her eyes firmly shut.

"You're doing great, Grace," said Addie. As they continued crawling along the small tunnel, Addie found herself telling Grace all about her mom. Grace was so absorbed in what Addie was saying that she began to forget where she was.

When Addie ran out of things to talk about, she asked Grace to teach her the school song. By the time they reached the other side of the tunnel they were both singing it at the top of their lungs.

# CHAPTER FIVE

"Stand up and open your eyes, Grace. You did it!" said Addie. "Great job!"

"I can't believe it!" said Grace.

Grace gave Addie a big hug. "Thanks so much! I guess your mom was right after all."

"It's a good trick," Addie agreed. "I was doing it going through that wormhole."

"That's why you had your eyes closed!" said Grace.

"Yes, I was pretty scared and it helped," said Addie. She glanced back into the tunnel.

"Grace, I was thinking about those aliens in the tunnel. They're oozing that orange sticky stuff and are really sick. They look even worse than the aliens on the other side of the mountain. They don't have much air in there, and what they do have is polluted."

"But what can we do?" said Grace.

"What about fresh air?" Addie suggested.

"Our tanks will be getting low soon if they aren't already," Grace pointed out. "We can't breathe this polluted air either."

"But maybe we don't need two oxygen poppers," said Addie, grinning.

"What are you thinking?" Grace asked.

"Well, if we popped one in the tunnel, the oxygen bubble would block the hole off for a while," said Addie. "It would stop the bad air from getting in, and the plant-like aliens could breathe in the oxygen and get better."

"We are only supposed to use them in an emergency," said Grace.

"What's going on in that tunnel is an emergency," Addie said. "And we'd still have yours if we popped mine. We can share one bubble." Addie pulled out her popper and her purple tutu came out with it. Addie tried to stuff it back in, but it was caught in the zipper of her mission pack. "Great!" she said, and she left it hanging.

"Put your popper away. We'll use mine for the aliens," said Grace.

"Are you sure?" Addie asked.

"Yep. I'm sure. I trust you," Grace said as she pointed her popper into the cave and pulled the cord.

"The tunnel is sealed off," said Grace. "The gas is thick over here. We must be close to it."

The girls moved through the blue aliens, listening to their noises and whispers. Then they came to a sudden stop and hid behind a pile of vine-like aliens. Not too far in front of them, all the blue life forms were gone. In their place was what looked like a factory. Five huge robots guarded it.

"I've seen those bots on a mission before," whispered Grace. "They're industroborgs. Factory bots. This factory is making something that produces all that green gas. I wish I knew what they were making inside."

"We have X-ray vision on our goggles," said Addie as she took the remote for her goggles from her mission pack. "You keep your goggles set to smoke screen so you can keep an eye on the borgs. I'll switch to X-ray view."

She pressed the button for X-ray view. Suddenly it was as if the factory walls weren't there. She could see everything inside. "They're making industroborgs," she told Grace. "It looks like it's all done by computer."

"So, if we can get to that computer we can stop everything," said Grace.

"Yes, but we have to get past the borgs first," said Addie. "Should we bring up Mrs. Lamrock on our watch holographs?"

"No. Let's watch for a minute," said Grace.

Addie switched her goggles back to smoke screen so she could see what was going on outside the building. The girls sat behind the pile of vine-like aliens and watched the five industroborgs. Two were spraying green gas at anything blue that came near the factory. Another two were guarding the factory's side walls. The last borg was guarding the entrance.

"I think the aliens could help us," said Grace. "We need to distract that borg guarding the door."

WWwEEEEellING

WooOOooARRRRRR

"My SpaceBerry is still on," said Addie. "They heard us."

"What are they saying?" asked Grace.

"To get ready," answered Addie.

"For what?" asked Grace.

Suddenly there was a loud rustling in the jungle on the far side of the factory. Vines and roots were thrashing around.

The industroborg guarding the doors heard the noise and looked over to where it was coming from. It marched off into the jungle to investigate.

"Now's our chance," said Grace.

Both girls raced into the factory.

It was filled with fully automated bot-making machinery, conveyor belts, and contraptions the girls had never seen before. There were different levels and lots of metal stairs going to and from them.

"I know where the computer is," yelled Addie over the noise. "Follow me."

She raced along a walkway that looked down on some conveyor belts and machines. Grace was right behind her.

Then Addie heard Grace scream. She turned around and saw Grace falling from the walkway. Grace landed on a fast-moving conveyor belt on the level below.

"Get off there!" cried Addie, seeing that the belt was heading for a machine that inserted metal industroborg arms.

"I can't," Grace cried. "I'm stuck!"

Addie could see that there were lots of metal borg arms on the conveyor belt. Looking around wildly, she saw a set of stairs. She ran down them and along to where Grace was struggling to get up.

"Grab my hands," Addie yelled as she ran along beside her. "I'll pull you off."

She bent farther over the belt to get a

better grip on Grace. Then she felt something pulling at her waist. "Oh no," Addie yelled. "My tutu is caught on the conveyor belt."

She was dragged along as the conveyor belt ate up more and more of the tutu's netting. Then the conveyor belt stopped.

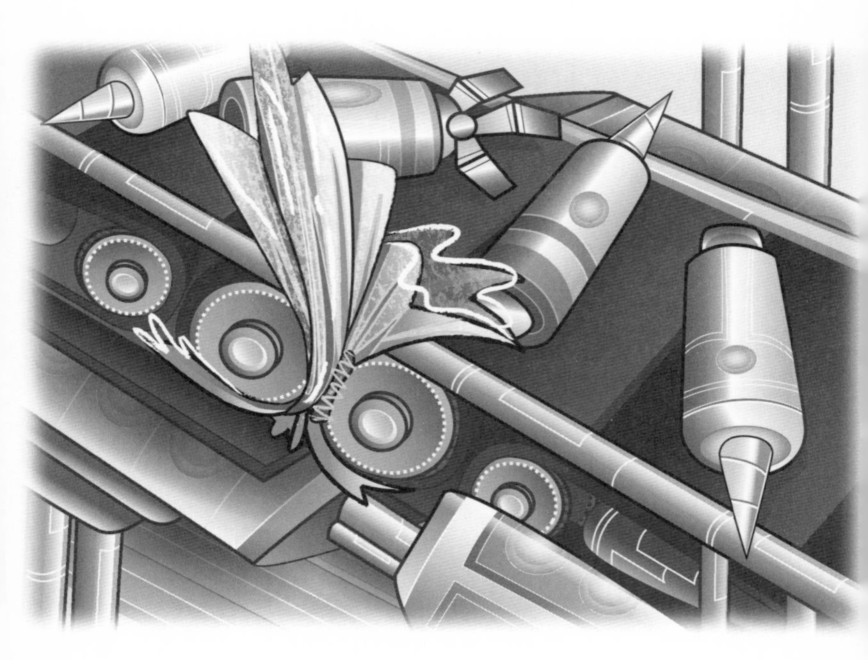

Addie looked down. All of her purple tutu was wrapped around the motor of the conveyor belt. The machine was broken.

Addie pulled Grace's arms, and Grace finally came free and climbed off the belt.

"Hooray for purple tutus!" Grace said. "Let's grab the computer and get out of here."

Addie led Grace back up the stairs and over to where a clear box held the computer that operated the factory. Addie smashed the box with her space boot and pulled the computer out. "Let's smash it too," she said, and they both jumped on it with their heavy space boots until it was in pieces.

Everything in the factory went still. They had stopped it.

"I hope the computer operated the industroborgs too," said Addie.

The girls walked through the quiet factory to the door and peered out. The industroborgs were completely still.

"We deactivated them," said Grace. "We did it! Time to call Space Surfer."

"And say goodbye to our beautiful blue friends," said Addie.

"And your purple tutu!" Grace laughed.

Grace took out her SpaceBerry and contacted Space Surfer.

"Be there in five minutes," Space Surfer replied.

# CHAPTER SIX

"Welcome home, girls," said Mrs. Lamrock. "What a successful mission you had. Congratulations! Oh, and well done for using the translator application. Points to both of you for downloading it."

"How do you already know about the app?" asked Addie. "We told Space Surfer a lot of things on the way home, but we didn't tell him about that."

"Did you forget about your watches?" asked Mrs. Lamrock.

"They were loaded with that new device that allowed us to listen in."

"Oh," said Grace looking disappointed. "That's right. We forgot all about that, Addie."

"Well, it worked up to a point and then we lost you," said Mrs. Lamrock.

"Really?" said Addie. "I mean, uhm, that's too bad. When did it drop out?"

"Not long after you entered the small tunnel," said Mrs. Lamrock. "Being under the mountain must have affected the reception, and it never worked again after that."

Addie squeezed Grace's hand. "We stopped the factory by smashing the computer," she said to Mrs. Lamrock. "And we had help from the life forms on Plantagan."

"Yes, and without needing the help of the holographic teacher. Well done, both of you," said Mrs. Lamrock. "High points earned there. We've sent a team in to remove the factory and everything in it. The air on Plantagan has already greatly improved."

"I need to get back to my dorm room," said Grace, looking a little glum. "Thanks, Mrs. Lamrock, and thanks for a great mission, Addie. You rock!"

"Wait, Comet XS," said Mrs. Lamrock. "You both earned bonus points on this mission. Don't you want to hear about them?"

Addie still had hold of Grace's hand and pulled her back. "Of course she does," she told Mrs. Lamrock.

"Bonus points for saving the Plantagan creatures in the cave," said Mrs. Lamrock. "Very clever. Bonus points are awarded also for working with the Plantagan creatures. Most importantly, bonus points are rewarded for both of you working together and facing your fears."

"Both of us?" said Grace.

"Particularly you, Comet XS," said Mrs. Lamrock. "Facing fear takes a lot of courage, and space agents need that quality." Then she turned to Addie. "This mission might just get you on the Cadet Scoreboard, Star Girl. We'll see. Off you go now, girls. Dinner has just started in the dining hall. I'm sure you're both hungry after your trip."

"Yes, Mrs. Lamrock," said Grace with a big smile on her face.

Addie and Grace arrived in the dining hall halfway through dinner. Everyone was busy eating.

"Grace," called Valentina. "Come and sit with us. I hope I'm back in the number one spot after your mission. I scored well on my trip yesterday. You guys scored a zero, I bet."

"Come with me," Grace said to Addie. "There's something I want to tell Valentina."

"Oh, no," said Addie. "You go. I'm okay. I'm going to go over and sit with Miya."

"No," said Grace. "Come with me, and then we'll both go and sit with Miya."

The girls walked over to where Valentina and her friends were sitting.

"Hello, Valentina," said Grace. "We had a really successful mission. Bonus points and everything! Addie was great. Mrs. Lamrock was right. At the FlyBy she said not everything is as it seems. On the outside I saw what I thought was a boring old school space shuttle, but on the inside it was amazing. I got the inside wrong with you too. You aren't so amazing after all."

Valentina looked a little flustered and turned her back on both of them.

After dinner Addie curled up on her bed in her dorm room.

"Sorry about your favorite tutu, Addie," Miya said from her bed. "When you go home on break, maybe you can get another one."

"It's okay. I'm so glad I had it with me in the end. Anyway, I think I kinda like this pink tutu Ms. Styles left on my bed for me," Addie said. "And I think I might check out the spaceball team. Ms. Styles left a note about it with my tutu."

"Good plan," said Miya. "Good night."

"Don't let the bed bugs bite!" said Addie. "I'm just going to send Dad a message, and then I'll turn the light out."

**ADDIE**

Hey Dad, How R U? I still miss home but getting better. Good friends and lots of fun here.

**DAD**

All good here. Glad it's getting better. Your mom would be so proud of you.

**ADDIE**

LOL you always say that. CYA Dad xoxo

**DAD**

CYA Ads, my extra special space cadet xoxo

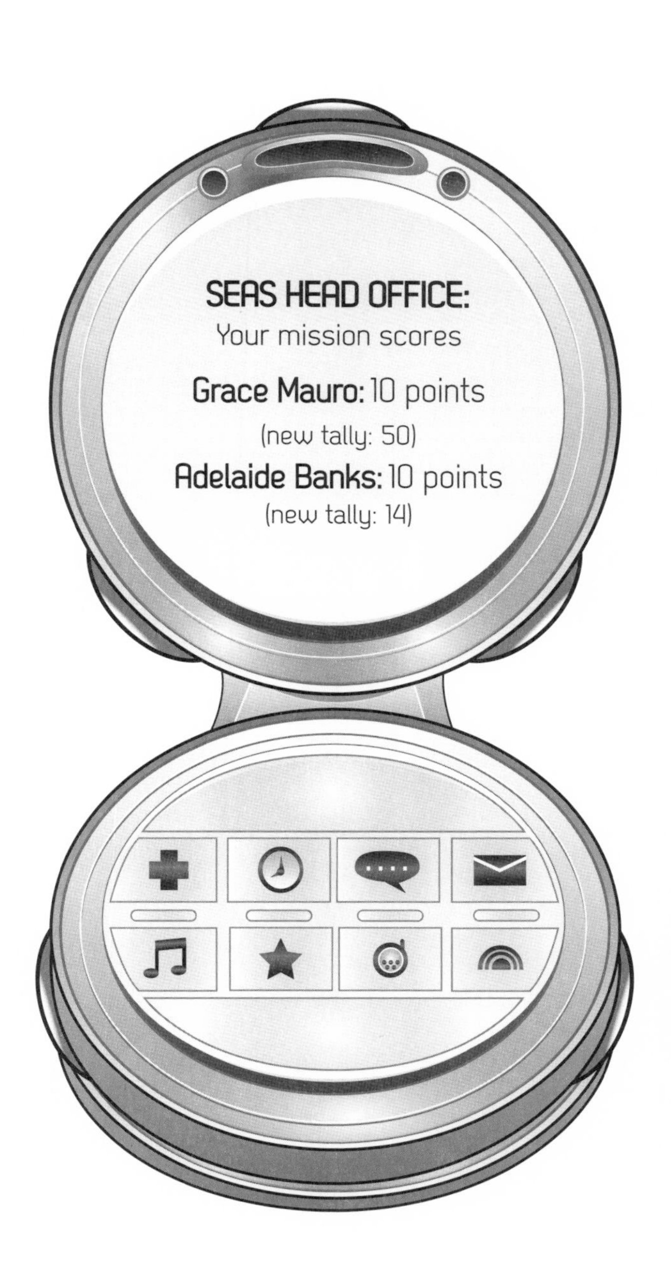
SEAS HEAD OFFICE:
Your mission scores
Grace Mauro: 10 points
(new tally: 50)
Adelaide Banks: 10 points
(new tally: 14)

# TOP TEN SPACE CADET SCOREBOARD

| NAME | PHOTO | CADET POINTS | HOUSE |
|---|---|---|---|
| Grace Mauro (SC Comet XS) | | 50 | NEBULA |
| Valentina Adams (SC Supernova 1) | | 45 | NEBULA |
| Louisa Jeffries (SC Star Cluster) | | 40 | NOVA |
| Hannah Merrington (SC Galactic 6) | | 38 | METEOR |
| Aziza Van De Walt (SC Asteroid) | | 35 | NOVA |
| Miyako Wakuda (SC Astron Girl) | | 34 | NOVA |
| Sabrina Simcic (SC Neuron Star) | | 30 | NEBULA |
| Lara Walsh (SC Red Giant) | | 28 | METEOR |
| Olivia Marston (SC Orbital 2) | | 24 | STELLAR |
| Adelaide Banks (SC Star Girl) | | 14 | STELLAR |

SCHOOL HOUSE SCOREBOARD

1st PLACE

NOVA

points: 288

2nd PLACE

NEBULA

points: 275

3rd PLACE

METEOR

points: 221

4th PLACE

STELLAR

points: 186

# STAR GIRL

## SAVING SPACE ONE PLANET AT A TIME

Check out all of Star Girl's space adventures!